A Note to Parents and Caregivers:

Read-it! Readers are for children who are just starting on the amazing road to reading. These beautiful books support both the acquisition of reading skills and the love of books.

 The PURPLE LEVEL presents basic topics and objects using high frequency words and simple language patterns.

 The RED LEVEL presents familiar topics using common words and repeating sentence patterns.

 The BLUE LEVEL presents new ideas using a larger vocabulary and varied sentence structure.

 The YELLOW LEVEL presents more challenging ideas, a broad vocabulary, and wide variety in sentence structure.

 The GREEN LEVEL presents more complex ideas, an extended vocabulary range, and expanded language structures.

 The ORANGE LEVEL presents a wide range of ideas and concepts using challenging vocabulary and complex language structures.

When sharing a book with your child, read in short stretches, pausing often to talk about the pictures. Have your child turn the pages and point to the pictures and familiar words. And be sure to reread favorite stories or parts of stories.

There is no right or wrong way to share books with children. Find time to read with your child, and pass on the legacy of literacy.

Adria F. Klein, Ph.D.
Professor Emeritus
California State University
San Bernardino, California

Editor: Jill Kalz
Designers: Joe Anderson and Hilary Wacholz
Page Production: Brandie Shoemaker
Art Director: Nathan Gassman
Associate Managing Editor: Christianne Jones
The illustrations in this book were created digitally.

Picture Window Books
5115 Excelsior Boulevard
Suite 232
Minneapolis, MN 55416
877-845-8392
www.picturewindowbooks.com

Printed in the United States of America.

Library of Congress Cataloging-in-Publication Data
Shaskan, Trisha Speed, 1973–
This is Anna / by Trisha Speed Shaskan ; illustrated by Burak Senturk.
p. cm. — (Read-it! readers)
Summary: The reader slowly discovers who Anna is as she draws a picture of herself.
ISBN-13: 978-1-4048-3168-1 (library binding)
ISBN-10: 1-4048-3168-1 (library binding)
ISBN-13: 978-1-4048-1244-4 (paperback)
ISBN-10: 1-4048-1244-X (paperback)
[1. Portraits—Fiction. 2. Self-perception—Fiction. 3. Individuality—Fiction.]
I. Senturk, Burak, 1973– ill. II. Title.
PZ7.S53242Th 2006
[E]—dc22   2006027297

This Is
Anna

by Trisha Speed Shaskan
illustrated by Burak Senturk

Special thanks to our advisers for their expertise:

Adria F. Klein, Ph.D.
Professor Emeritus, California State University
San Bernardino, California

Susan Kesselring, M.A.
Literacy Educator
Rosemount–Apple Valley–Eagan (Minnesota) School District

PiCTURE WiNDOW BOOKS
Minneapolis, Minnesota

This is Anna. Anna has long hair.

Anna has long, wavy brown hair.

Anna wears a necklace.

Anna wears a necklace with three emeralds on it.

Anna wears a dress.

Anna wears a purple dress with ruffles on the sleeves.

Anna wears stockings.

Anna wears bright red-and-white striped stockings.

Anna wears shoes.

Anna wears silver shoes with large square buckles.

Anna wears a robe.

Anna wears a dark red robe with fake fur trim.

Anna sits on a throne.

Anna sits on a fancy throne made
of gold.

Anna holds a cat.

Anna holds a white cat wearing
a blue and green collar.

Anna wears a crown.

Anna wears a tall crown with three emeralds and nine rubies on it.

This is Princess Anna!

More *Read-it!* Readers

Bright pictures and fun stories help you practice your reading skills. Look for more books at your level.

Ann Plants a Garden
The Babysitter
Bess and Tess
The Best Soccer Player
Coco on the Go
Dan Gets Set
Fishing Trip
Jen Plays
Joey's First Day
Just Try It
Mary's Art
The Missing Tooth
Moving Day
Pat Picks Up
A Place for Mike
Room to Share
Shopping for Lunch
Syd's Room
Tricky Twins

Looking for a specific title or level? A complete list of *Read-it!* Readers is available on our Web site:
www.picturewindowbooks.com